Populati

Ersto DiBaggio

This work is licensed under a Creative Commons Attribution-ShareAlike 3.0 Unported License. This means you are free to share, sell, modify, and create derivative works, so long as you credit the original authors and release your work under the same license.

Part of the Ascension Epoch
http://www.ascensionepoch.cc

Contents

Contents 2
In Hoc Signo 3
The Lost Boy 15
The Devil to Pay 22
The Lights Go Out 31
Appendix - The Signalman 38
Gallery 39
About the Ascension Epoch 43
About the Creators 45

In Hoc Signo

Journal of Jamison Doyle
13 July, 1898

I enter the following account without hesitation, though any who should read it may think me a liar or else insensible, drunk, or delirious from facing that monstrous power that drives man toward extinction. But such awesome events as I have witnessed demand chronicling regardless of the risk to my reputation. Against such things as I have witnessed (whose very existence humbles my puny intellect and flames my weakling spirit to heights undreamt), the strength of all ridicule, mockery, and self-doubt fails. If I lie or even exaggerate, then the Devil take me, for I cannot conceive of a sin more wicked than to besmirch this miracle with the patina of falsehood. Take these words as the truth and nothing but.

It started yesterday, the twelfth, when I was roused by Jack McDonald, the inspector of track of the Severn Valley line and an old family acquaintance who had worked with my father. I had not seen him for more than a decade, and yet I recognized the same alert face and confident bearing I remembered as a youth. He reported that he had come from speaking to Mr. Palfrey and had obtained his permission, if I were willing, to take me to Arley. That beleaguered rail line had fallen under his responsibility and he was in dire need of men to replace those lost either to enemy action or cowardice, and he explained how very important it was to maintain the service with so many fleeing from the enemy's onslaught in the north.

I assented immediately, though I was, I am ashamed to admit, sorely tempted to abandon my duties and flee for some safe harbor (presuming such a place now exists on this embattled earth). I was inspired by the courage and nobility of this stalwart gentleman, still putting the lives of others above his own even in this grim predicament, and I told him so. Mr. McDonald, being too humble a man to be comfortable with compliments, hurried onto the matter of what urgent tasks needed doing. In the course of this, he intimated the surprising extent of his manpower shortage and the great wreck of the whole valley: of more than a hundred men that he regularly supervised, fewer than a dozen were available for work. Some had definitely perished, but of others he knew nothing.

The evidence of the depopulation and ruin was only too evident as we traveled northward, and I, who had been spared the worst in the relative calm of Cheltenham, was shocked by the empty ruins of what had been vibrant towns and cities. When the wild rumor emerged that the Crown and Parliament had fled from the isles for the fastness of India, fear imposed such an eagerness to leave in her subjects that they brought only what they could carry in one trip. There were many spots along the roads where provisions and private effects had been abandoned, perhaps to make room for another desperate passenger.

And all the time we traveled northward, so the invaders drove south.

At one o' clock this morning, I was awakened by McDonald, who informed me that an hour before, what was evidently a small scouting force of the enemy sent to probe the strength of our resistance had penetrated deep into the country and had demolished miles of track above Victoria Bridge before being driven off by artillery fire. All telegraph lines were down and no warning could be made to a train of evacuees departing Shropshire, which would derail to the doom of all unless they could be warned off.

I dressed quickly, donning my high boots and Mackintosh (for the rain was then in a downpour) and brought my signaling lantern. We hastened northwest by a rickety one-horse carriage, the only transport left to us in this devastated area. Eventually we came to a spot that would admit no passage for our vehicle, the trail ending at a rocky slope by the track which cleaved tightly to the bend of the hillside, and so dismounted. There we waited, straining our ears for the sound of the cranking wheels or the steam whistle, for our lamp shed little light on the oily night, and we dared not illuminate the electric signal beacon before the train approached for fear of attracting the attention of some distant inhuman war engine.

God knows how long we waited. In the quaking fear of our grim anticipation, either of the train's absence or of our own fearful discovery by the alien foe, there could be no reckoning of time. The impenetrable, moonless dark seemed the timeless chaos before creation.

Whenever it was that we heard the blast of the train's whistle in the distance, my heart leapt for joy. The train had not been destroyed! Jack shook my shoulder excitedly, evidently feeling the same sense of elation. What a profound kinship with his fellow sufferers despair engenders in man, so that even moment to moment survival seemed like a great victory, a thing almost too dear to be hoped for!

Oh, but how my heart sank when that whistle was silenced by the keening wail of the Tripod guns!

The groaning of yielding steel and the thunderous roar that I knew to be the rupture of the locomotive engine echoed down the valley, and tongues of yellow and orange flame spouted around the bend, igniting the trees on the hillside. It was in this ghastly light that the corpse of the train came into view, still barreling forward under its gigantic momentum. The hurtling wreck was pursued by a brace of the Martian war machines striding athwart the incline, their hideously pulsing, spindly legs mastering the terrain with unnatural grace.

"God save their souls! Let's go! Let's go! Oh, it's too late for them!" McDonald urged me, for stout and dedicated though he was, the hopelessness of the sight unmanned him.

But I could not heed his words. It was as if my body was petrified, and I had no choice but to watch the slaughter unfold. I was beyond the reach of fear or rage. It was the sheer spectacle of the thing that held me, mute and transfixed, mesmerized by the dance of the fire light, the wall of heat, and the cacophony of death.

"What is that?" I pointed to a new source of illumination on the hillside, a roiling ball of blue-green light hovering above the flaming train. It seemed to be darting fire at the tripods, and the machines alternated their volleys between it and the slowing locomotive. The bursts were as bright as lightning, shifting the rainy night into daytime brightness with every crackling burst. The tripod on the left groaned and collapsed under this attack, its leg sheared off at the pivot as its pilot housing released great gouts of fire. The machine on the right seemed to be mortally wounded too, spewing copious amounts of smoke. Belatedly I realized that the inky cloud that oozed out was not smoke, but the lethal chemical these machines belched out to inflict the widest possible havoc on the concentrated masses of helpless city dwellers. I knew, somehow, that this was an act of desperation.

The combatants continued their duel until a swarm of buzzing, explosive bomblets burst from the remaining Tripod and overwhelmed the fighting nimbus. It crashed to earth well in front of the train, smashing the timber and rails of the track until it tumbled down the embankment. The blue-green light faded and the embers of the burning forest were hid by the veil of the Black Smoke.

"Good God, Doyle, hurry before they get us!" McDonald warned, but again I did not heed him. As I instead headed toward the carnage, toward the poisonous smoke, I heard him call, "Where are you going, you damned fool!"

I myself wondered what had possessed me. I admit now that it was desperation and hopelessness. I was sorely tired of running, hiding, and waiting for death, and I damned those vicious creatures to do their worst. I was enlivened by the fight that intrepid phantasm had given them. Whoever it was – for at the time I thought it was a man, some scientific promethean with the ingenuity and boldness to harness electricity into a weapon great enough to put fear into these unstoppable foes – had reminded me that I had a duty to carry out, and carry it out I should, even though it meant my death. I resolved to see to the safety of any survivors, God willing, starting with that valiant Icarus.

I, too, had electricity at my command as I soon remembered, and lifting it above my head, I ignited the electric signal beacon to give light to my steps and, in a feeble way, to challenge the Martians. How vain! How foolish! And yet this futile gesture gave me inspiration and courage.

I followed the trail of the crash several yards down the hillside, grimly eyeing the viscous folds of the approaching cloud at the margins of my lantern as I descended. The trail of destruction ended abruptly and it seemed that there was nothing left of the wondrous flying machine and its pilot. But then I heard a voice call out; no, not in my ears, but between them. It was like a thought out loud. How else shall I describe it?

"Hasten to me!" it commanded, and I obeyed, somehow able to track this silent voice to its source.

In a pit gouged into the earth amid the scorched and smoldering leaves reposed a being not easily viewed and less easily described. It was neither man nor machine as I had suspected. Its form exceeded by far the alienness of the scrambling, spiderish bodies of the invaders – or of anything else that might conceivably arise in the wildest diversity of the natural world!

(This last observation was formed quite apart from rational evaluation. It was a truth comprehensible only to that exalted part of man's mind not made of the rude stuff of dust and ash, but that divine organ that perceives all things in perfect clarity, and this knowledge is as terrible and majestic as the thing before which I now cowered.)

It seemed, at first, a pattern of light, like the illusion one sees on the back of his eyelids after the flashbulb, only it was not disordered, but a regular, discreet pattern, like an unfathomably complex snowflake. Nor was it monochrome, but a riot of colors, especially warm shades of amber and crimson, with splinters of the stark blue of electric arcs.

As I stared at this wonder, my whole attention and thought seemed to be drawn into it, and with this new focus I began to discern a form more definitely animate and more terrible.

Its torso was gigantic and powerfully thewed, like a colossus carved from granite, though its configuration and musculature could hardly be less human. Its smooth hide glittered with the motion of hundreds of dilating, many-hued irises, each encircling a golden pupil. Six corded arms radiated from its center, branching and re-branching until they covered a span three or four times as wide as its height, stretching a taut, gossamer membrane, burnt and punctured from the battle, between them. It had no legs, and indeed the bottom half of this giant figure seemed to have been sheared off (undoubtedly by the enemy heat rays) at an acute angle delineated by charred lines from which seeped a glistening amber ichor. The head, most startlingly, had three faces; one human, one leonine, and one with the pointed beak and broad eyes of a bird of prey. It was not connected to the thing's body as it should have been, but instead floated inches above, rotating its faces as it addressed me in soundless words.

"Fear not! I am Eldil. I have come for your strengthening, not your chastisement," the entity declared, its tone surpassingly and incongruously mild against its fearsome aspect.

At the creature's command, the animal fear that threatened to unman me burned away, replaced with a wonder that could only be born of supernal grandeur.

The human head, with drooping eyes, enjoined me to bless him.

With tremulous hands, I made the sign of the cross and recited a hushed and hurried prayer. "Heavenly Father, shed your grace and mercy upon us and shield this soul in the hour of peril."

"He hears, even on this silent world! My long watch is ended and I depart, but into your hands I pass the Azure Lens. It will fortify your body and enliven your mind with wisdom. With it, bring courage to the afflicted."

The Lion-head followed in a roaring bellow: "Receive also the Crimson Lens; it will magnify His wrath, bringing justice to the iniquitous. Vanquish evil with it, but attempt no evil with it, or it will consume you!"

"Behold the Golden Lens!" cried the aquiline aspect. "It will amplify your senses and speed your journeys, even through the deeps of heaven and the bastions of the Walls Between."

"Wield these in my place. Defend your people," said the human voice.

"I will," I affirmed, finding that no other answer was possible.

The oily haze of the lethal Martian gas reached us, dampening the light. My skin prickled where the residue touched it and the toxic vapor seared my eyes and blistered my throat and lungs as I breathed it. I hacked and wheezed, helplessly drawing in more of the deadly substance. Every nerve screamed out in pain, and I was certain that I would accompany this creature to the next world, but then the creature spoke and its three voices outsounded my death throes.

"Know neither fear, nor malice, nor despair!"

Three arms – long, sinewy human arms – spun into existence before my very eyes, each gripping a thick, convex disc alive with ordered swirls and pulses of light: azure, crimson, and gold. I saw dimly, through a haze of tears, the ephemeral limbs plunge into my chest. I heaved and shuddered, though now from a wholly different cause than the poison of the Black Smoke.

"Your soul is reforged in the crucible of the Celestial Fire, the light that warms forever!"

I fell to my hands and knees in the mud while the entity evaporated in the same manner its arms had materialized. Suddenly the whole world seemed to shift on its axis. A mighty exhale expelled the black oil from my lungs and a wreath of cerulean fire enveloped me, burning away the lethal haze.

Hand over foot, I ascended the slope, my left hand still dragging the signal lantern, though it had been transformed through some process into a new shape, its single signaling portal replaced with a triad of lenses streaming blue, red, and yellow light.

Filled with vigor and hope, I marshaled all of my determination and extended the nimbus of light that covered me to a breadth and height of many yards, lighting the surroundings like moon glow on the ocean and burning away all of the lethal fog.

I saw that the alien war machine noticed me, for its turreted head rotated its face towards me. The panels of its heat projector opened like a leering eye, gigantic and astonished. Its deadly gaze lingered on me as I strode toward it. At last, its panels glowed brilliantly and it discharged its incinerating beam.

I cannot articulate why I did not think to dodge its fire or seek cover in the ditch, I just know that I had no fear of the weapon and that I was so bent on its destruction that I did not want to delay my onset even

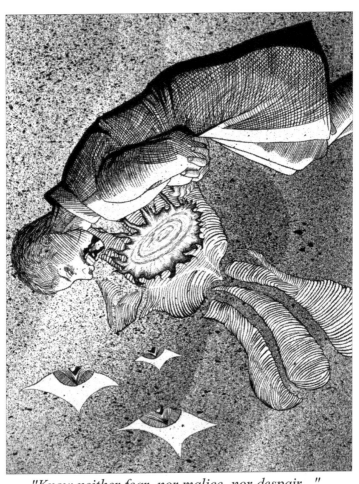

"Know neither fear, nor malice, nor despair..."
Shell Presto, 2012

for a second. My confidence was not misplaced, for its attack washed over the blue nimbus but did not touch me.

There was nothing left for me to do. I resolved upon its destruction and the enemy was destroyed. How can I explain the inexplicable? All of the indignation, the righteous rage provoked from the loss of all that these beasts had destroyed and all that they aimed to destroy, boiled out of the lantern in a scarlet fury, and the Tripod was no more.

I did not marvel as the death machine tumbled to the ground, but instead began searching for survivors in the wreckage of the train. I tore through great hunks of metal many times my weight to reach at bodies, many burnt, all of them lifeless. I walked upon the very air, ascending high and looking with eyes sharper than the keenest hawk, but there were no survivors, nor any trace of Jack McDonald. As he has not yet returned to his home, I can only hope, and pray, that he made good his escape.

Although I am mentally exhausted, my body is filled with an incredible stamina that will admit no rest. I can feel the Azure Lens burning inside me, urging me to the completion of my task, which is simply this: to repulse the invaders and liberate this good world. And the Lens counsels me wisely: just as this peril is not to one man alone, neither is humanity's defense. I will require allies, mighty, stalwart, and brilliant men, empowered perhaps even as I am. The Lens knows where to find them.

God willing, our victory is at hand.

Peter and the Fairies
Arthur Rackham, 1906

The Lost Boy

The streets of Woking were crowded that Saturday afternoon, much more so than usual owing to the commotion in the sandpits outside of town. There, the boffins and such folk as didn't have enough business of their own to mind had gathered to gawk at a great cast-iron capsule fallen from the sky. Some knaves chattered ridiculously that it had come from the planet Mars, and some others were fool enough to believe them. Most sensible people agreed that it was a shell launched by that giant German gun, a boast from the Kaiser that Her Majesty was sure to answer in a way not to the liking of her churlish grandson.

Then there were a few people who hardly gave a thought to such matters, and one of them was a young lady – let's call her Mary, as so many young ladies are, for no one knows her name for sure – a new mum, very pretty and proud of her baby boy, whom she pushed around in a cozy little pram. All her thoughts were on this little boy, who was born the previous Sunday eve, nearly a week old now, and was to be baptized tomorrow at old St. Peter's, the church of his namesake.

Now, it was generally believed to be bad luck to take a child out before he was baptized, but Mary wasn't raised to be superstitious, and this strong young girl had been cooped up in bed for too many days, and now that the weather was bright and sunny she felt she just must have some air, and it would do no good to go promenading without little Peter, since all of the neighbors would be asking about him. And she went alone, because her husband, a strapping young lieutenant in the 11th Hussars, had to be about on maneuvers.

Poor Mary might have been better off if she'd been a bit more superstitious, because she never made it home that day – or at least not the home she was expecting. But then again, many people in Woking who stayed in their homes and businesses fared no better, and expired in the flames or under collapsing timbers. It was the oily black smoke that did in Mary and her darling little boy, sadly unbaptized as I have already reported.

When the sun went down, the smoke had mostly cleared, and the bodies lay in the streets right where they first fell. For a little while there was no more commotion on the streets of Woking, and then, gradually, it returned. The rats came out, along with a few mewling cats to pester them. A riderless horse sometimes clopped by from the Common, and later on, when the moon rose high, mangy dogs with their stomachs clung to their ribs came on and had their unwholesome victuals. At midnight, the beasts were joined by other things that came around at such times as this, things without form or flesh – at least not the flesh you're used to. Things that men saw only with great difficulty; things that, in these days, most men dismissed even though their ancestors huddled around bonfires in fear of them.

Now some of these creatures came from the worlds sidewise to this one, moving in wispy black shrouds that might have been cloaks, with bone-white fingers wrapped around translucent scythes that cut loose the struggling spirit from its shackle of flesh. Others were golden hued and rosy cheeked, and they blew on flutes or plucked lyres, and those trepidatious souls who had not already shuffled off were charmed into following. Some they led to good destinations, and others to not so good ones, but the weak, sickly spirit of little Peter they passed by. That forlorn *numen* could barely even peek outside the prison of his own eyes, through which he could only dimly see the other dead folks go marching.

Deep into the night, some other creatures came by – clad in form and flesh somewhat more like what you're used to – and had a look around. They laughed a bit, and generally approved of the change.

"We haven't had a walk around here in quite a long time," one of them said. "It feels good to get my toes in this old dirt again."

"Yes, but they've made quite a mess of this place," said another.

Now these were wicked sounding words, but the creatures weren't really wicked, no more than a bear or a lion is wicked. Cruel, perhaps, and certainly savage, but they lacked that divinely bestowed discernment that made man culpable for his sins. These creatures were the Fey.

"It'll take a good long time to be put back to right," agreed a third. "*If* they don't come back."

And they all had a look around, and some of them thought that maybe this time the men really wouldn't come back. Then the world could return to what it used to be, back when it was still old, but young in their memory. For the Fey had lived in these isles when they were greener and more pleasant, before even the first brute men in shaggy cloaks trod across the dry English Channel.

A fairy of the *Airish* sort, a pixie with bright butterfly wings, fluttered over little Peter's body and, for the first time that night, someone paid him notice.

Now this pixie was a girl, or at least a girlish sort of Fey, for sex, like the other human qualities they adopted, was more of something they aped rather than something they really possessed. And she had learned to ape some other human qualities in line with her sex, like sympathy, affection, and even a desire for motherhood. Like all fairy qualities, even the positive ones, these were not fully wholesome attributes, and so she didn't react to the sight of poor Peter's suffocating spirit the way a human would have. Instead, she felt a selfish delight, like a child who finds a discarded toy in the rubble of a burned down house.

"Come out, little boy!" she cooed as she bent down to his prison, and beckoned him out with her finger. Out rose his weakling spirit, slowly, cautiously. A breath of sweetness, a struggling flicker of light, an echo – little Peter's *numen* was none of these things, but might remind you of each of them.

"That won't do, little boy!" she giggled. "Don't you know what you are? Don't you know how to behave?"

The fairy danced around him and waved her arms and her wings, and he floated up like a feather. She teased and she breathed, she thought, and weaved, and pulled, and then little Peter's *numen* was not a breath or an echo or a flicker of light anymore, but a definite shape and solidity, the makings of a body perhaps like the one he might have had if he had not choked on the black smoke, a body made of the same tenuous matter as the fey girl. Through the long night she helped him grow, and his head was covered with wild brown hair, and his clever eyes had color. And then, discovering he had a voice, he laughed with pure joy.

This little explosion sent the fairy reeling, and she felt as if she might grow herself, or sprout a new pair of wings. She laughed and cheered and scooped up Peter into her arms, cradling him against her bosom like his own mother might.

This racket didn't go unnoticed, and some of the other Fey gathered to see what had happened. Most of them quickly lost interest, as they did with most things, but the few who stayed looked on disapprovingly. But whether their disapproval grew from a sense of violated propriety or from jealousy, no one can really say.

A satyr called out to the pixie, whose name in the Fey language sounded like the tinkling of a tiny, silver bell, and asked just what she thought she was doing.

"I've found a little boy! His name is Peter. He'll be my son now, and I'll be his mother," she replied.

"You know you can't do that, it'll be the end of you! Leave him where you found him, for the psychopomps will be looking for him," the other said.

"I can do what I want! This one hasn't gone down to drown in the bright water, and the psychopomps already passed him over. He's my son, and I am his mother now!"

The satyr's stern face frowned in disagreement. "That's a man child. You'll never be his mother."

And the fairy whose name sounded like the chiming of a tiny bell stomped her foot and shouted. "Fine! Who needs a mother, anyway? Nevertheless, he's coming back with me, and we will do things that you've never imagined." The pixie went about her business, picking through the rubble for things her little boy might like: a toy wooden sword, a peacock feather from a lady's hat. In a flash of inspiration, she decided that he would need stories for his bedtime reading. In the ruins of a bookseller, she picked two volumes at random – not that it mattered, since she couldn't read anyway – *A General History of the Pyrates* and *Song of Hiawatha*.

The satyr looked on and said nothing, but he was very troubled. No human child had ever been brought to their country, but he had heard of the trouble they caused whenever one had come to other realms in the Dreamscape. He had heard dreadful stories of how their minds, every bit as mercurial and capricious as the Fey, altered the very stuff of the Dreamscape at their whim, transforming it until there was nothing recognizable – until there was no room left for the Fey. In other words, just like the way things were *here*. Did she want there to be no place left for the Fey anywhere in Tellus? The satyr said all these things to her.

"I don't care! I will do what I want, and so will he! And if there's no place left for you, then it will be even better!" She laughed spitefully. "But I'll give him your name so we can remember you when you're gone! Peter Pan, I'll call him!"

Dawn was coming, and there was no time left to dawdle; the gates of the Rampart were closing. The pixie soared into the twilight. Nestled in her arms, little Peter's eyes were filled with mischief and cunning as he bid good bye to the world of his birth.

Cyclone Ranger
Shell Presto, 2014

The Devil to Pay

It was the ninth day of Oak Creek's captivity when Lobo and his bandits led a new prisoner into the canyon. Those few citizens of the small Arizona mining town still around to talk about it were in a commotion, their eyes gawking and their voices full of fear and anticipation. As he squinted over the heads of the small crowd, Clarence Gibson didn't see much to fuss over, and when he replaced his eyeglasses he thought the newcomer looked even less remarkable. The prisoner looked as hollow and bedraggled as everyone else, and quite as helpless, too, as the fat bearded Mexican buffeted him with the butt of his rifle. The stranger was chained at the wrists and at the ankles so he couldn't balance himself; he fell over limply in the dirt and then slowly wormed his way to the smooth face of the rock wall and sat, his shoulders slumped and head bowed against his knees.

"That's him, I tell you!" Joshua Cobb whispered excitedly to a younger boy. "Harken to that long black coat and the black blindfold!"

Clarence hadn't noticed the blindfold. He took off his glasses and tried to wipe the dust away, but his white shirt was yellowing with a week's worth of sweat and dirt, and he only succeeded in smudging them. He hobbled toward the small gathering, leaning hard on the cane in his right hand.

"You speak as if you haven't seen a man in a frock coat before, Joshua," said Clarence. "Who do you think he is?"

"It's the Devil Rider, Mr. Gibson! It's more than just the coat, sir, it's the way he wears it, and that fancy gun belt I saw the Mexicans take from him." Joshua replied.

"The Devil Rider," sniffed Clarence. "Frontier superstition!"

"No sir!" The young man took off his hat and held it in front of him, hands crossed, the way he used to stand at recitation in Clarence's schoolroom. "Ain't no normal man that walks around blind-folded, yet can see!"

"*Isn't*, Joshua. The word is *isn't*." Clarence corrected him with a twinge of irritation.

"Why does he wear such a thing?" asked the younger boy, Joshua's interlocutor.

"They say that he was captured by Apaches and staked out to die in the desert, and the savages cut off his eyelids so he couldn't shield his eyes from the sun. He died and went to Hell, but he was too wild for the Devil and so he was sent back, but his eyes were burnt and useless, so he uses the blindfold to walk unnoticed among normal people."

"My word!" exclaimed the younger boy's mother.

"And how does he see without eyes?" pressed the lad.

"Well, the Devil put a ghostly red fire in his eye sockets, which he can see through by some form of witchcraft – or so it is said. Also that he has the keenest hearing and the strength of ten men, and never misses when he fires. And some folks call him the Cyclone Ranger, for the Devil set a terrible storm to follow wherever he goes, and it carries the souls of the damned to Hell. But those flaming eyes are only visible at night when they shine through the blindfold. That much is certain."

Clarence smiled condescendingly at the youth. "My, my! You're certain about a lot of things you've never seen yourself, aren't you? Even Satan's own motives!"

"I've heard enough. You must have too, though I know you don't have truck with such talk," said Joshua sheepishly.

"I have, indeed. I have heard that he was sent back to punish the wicked – isn't that right? Now why would the Devil want to do that?"

"Well shucks, Mr. Gibson, what else does the Devil do but just that?" rejoined Joshua, to the murmuring approval of others.

Clarence frowned, chagrined that what he had thought to be a decisive blow was so deftly turned round on him.

"The Rider's bound duty is to hunt down all the murderers and thieves and rascals in the west and hasten them to Hell," Joshua went on, encouraged. "And that's exactly what he's done – to the Glancy boys, and the Stirling gang, and they say it was he that last year found mean George Coney in a saloon and shot him crippled and then left him to strangle from the ceiling fan until *his* eyeballs popped out of *his* head!"

"That'll do, Joshua Cobb!" the younger boy's mother interjected, clamping her hands over her son's ears. "Ethan's got enough to worry about without you filling his head with tales of devils and popped-out eyeballs!"

"I'm right sorry, Mrs. Gray," Joshua apologized, but his voice was cheerful, almost exuberant. "But I reckon that's just what he's doing here! Come to bring justice to these bandits and send those other wretched things back to Hell – or Mars, or wherever it is they come from!"

"Huh! Well maybe he is the Devil Rider, but he ain't done much good so far, has he?" put in a dried-up old timer. "No guns, tied up like a hog and led around by them banditos! The Devil sure picks 'em poorly!"

There was a cluck of grim laughter and "hear, hears" of agreement as the gaggle broke up. But Clarence, still standing near, noted a different expression on many of their faces. Though they outwardly scoffed at Joshua's ghost story, they wanted to believe it.

The phantom hope was hard to hold onto. The day wore on in oppressive heat and then came the chill of the night air beneath the cloudless sky, bringing neither food nor a return of the men who had been taken as forced labor into the caves. The newcomer hardly stirred, not even to take their meager offerings food and water. Not once did he speak.

And then the next morning, Lobo returned.

The Mexican staggered toward them, hardly daring to pick his feet up off the dirt for fear of falling. He was stone drunk, but not from the rowdy carousing his band had often troubled the town with in better days. Since he returned to Oak Creek alongside the invaders, Lobo was in the bag every hour of the day, and he had the stink and look of a man who drank for numbness rather than celebration. Such skin as was visible on his hairy face was pallid and beaded with sweat and his left hand trembled visibly. The eyes that had once been in a perpetual squint of wild, boisterous mirth were now little glassy ovals floating on a fat pillow of sagging skin, always staring straight ahead. Every lively thing about him seemed to have been drowned, even his temper and lechery. Now when Lobo killed it was dispassionate, perfunctory, and Clarence no longer troubled with fears of the brute forcing himself on a lady, for he seemed to show no interest in them. The Mexican outlaw was still to be feared, but he had become so pathetic that Clarence now found it impossible to hate him.

The remnants of Oak Creek stood up and bunched together as their jailers neared. Clarence felt his neighbors' eyes on him. He squared his shoulders and swallowed his fear to do the manful thing that they expected of him as their spokesman.

"Have you brought food and clean water with you? We're running out of it. And we want news of the men that were led off from here," he called out, his voice shaky at the first.

Lobo shook his head, and his body wobbled precariously with it. "No food yet, *señor*."

"You cannot starve us to death! If you are not going to provide us the food and water, then as a Christian man, as a human being, you must release us."

Lobo shrugged his shoulders with great effort. "Soon this trouble will be over. But now, the conquerors have need of another man."

Low groaning went up from the captives.

"What men?" Clarence shouted, looking around frantically. "Most of the men had gone with the army before you got here, what remains you've already taken! All that is left are the old and infirm, and women and children! What has happened to the others?"

Lobo was not going to discuss it. His trembling arm shot out, a pudgy finger pointed at Joshua. "You, boy! Come!"

Four men with Winchester repeaters and shotguns muscled into the group to lay hands on the young man, and Clarence bravely stepped in front of them.

"No," he said, his voice low, but clear. "No. If the conquerors must have another man, then I will-" Clarence's declaration ended in a cry as a sallow-faced Mexican roughly grabbed him by the collar, kicked his cane out from under him and hurled him to the ground.

"Men, not cripples!" Lobo shouted viciously. "*Vamanos*!"

"Don't you worry, Mr. Gibson. I'll go, I ain't afraid of these rats!" said Joshua Cobb, struggling under the tight grip of his captors.

The women and the children were sobbing as they led him off, and Clarence's eyes also began to fill with tears as his thoughts filled with dread. In a dry and shaky voice, he called out: "For God's sake, why do you need more men? What happened to the others?"

From the bandits there was no answer, but heaven, perhaps, replied. The wind gusted and the sky turned suddenly drab and gray, the way that storms break in the desert. Somewhere yet far off there was a peal of thunder and it echoed off the canyon walls. The world now darkened the way Clarence's hopes had. He lay where he fell, injured and humiliated, and silently cursed his infirmities.

"You'd better take me, too," someone said, once the echo of the thunder had died.

Clarence's head rose and looked in the direction of the voice. It was clear and deep and steady. It reminded him of his older brother, Caleb, so much alike that he had to remind himself that Caleb had been dead for eight years. Where Clarence was weak, Caleb was strong, and where Clarence was timid, Caleb was brave.

For years he told himself that he had forgotten his brother's face, but the image returned to him, and it buoyed him, gave him enough strength to grab his cane and pull himself back onto his feet.

He saw that the words had come from the prisoner they'd brought in yesterday. The stranger was still shackled, his head still bowed, but now he was standing and his shoulders were not hunched but spread as broadly as the chains allowed. The blindfolded figure seemed to Clarence like a statue by one of the great renaissance sculptors: still, but poised with explosive potential. His physical presence was dominating, and it held Lobo and his henchmen rapt.

"Although I don't think your conquerors will much care for the type of man I am," the stranger spoke again.

Lobo spat. "You should thank God they've no use for the blind, fool!"

The blindfolded man stepped forward to the edge of the fence. "Is it that you don't know who I am, or that you don't believe?" He cocked his head toward Joshua. "The boy knows. He'll tell you."

Joshua took two halting steps backward as thunder again echoed in the distance and the sky grew darker. In the gathering gloom, the stranger's head rose for the first time, and a soft red glow as if from cooling embers shone beneath the blindfold.

Before Lobo could finish his blasphemous exclamation, the prisoner had burst his chains with a mighty heave of his arms and swung the broken links in a circle around his head, knocking one of the bandits senseless. The chain wrapped around the barrel of another's rifle and tore it from his hands. The stranger's trigger hand moved on the lever-action like a musician fretting a guitar, producing five deafening reports in quick succession. All of the bandits lay sprawled in the dirt, Lobo rolling around in the dust, eyes gawping, trying to press his fingers over the ragged hole torn through his throat.

It happened so quickly that Clarence, watching from a few yards distant, barely realized what had happened before the stranger was beside him, thrusting the rifle into his hand. The echo of the gunfire was still ringing in his ears as were the shocked cries of his fellow townsfolk. One voice in particular stood out from the cacophony.

"He is the Devil Rider! The Cyclone Ranger!" young Ethan Gray screamed.

Clarence looked up numbly into the fiery orbs that shined through the black blindfold. His mouth dropped open with a flash of unexpected recognition. "Ca-Caleb?"

"It's been a long time, Clarence," said Caleb Gibson.

"Caleb! Caleb! Thank Jesus! I was told you were dead!" Clarence threw himself onto his brother, showing the sort of affection he'd never shown before but vowed that he would if ever God were so good as to give him the chance again.

"You were told right, brother," Caleb said as he broke off their embrace. He gestured to the dead bandits. "Take their guns and lead everyone back to town, and whatever you do, don't look back."

"There are still some men in the mines," Clarence suggested.

"They're beyond anyone's help or hurt now, Clarence," Caleb replied. "Most of them are dead already, worked to death. Lobo's men have been burning them on the far ridge, along with the invaders who've fallen from sickness. The Martians fear the dead, ours and their own."

"God Almighty! Then where are you going? We all have to leave now, before those monsters come down here! They'll have heard the gunfire!"

The blindfolded man grinned. "Leave the monsters to me. They're dying, Clarence. They think there's a way home somewhere in this canyon, or maybe a way to bring more of their kind here. That's what they're digging for, but they won't find it."

"Don't be foolish, Caleb!" Clarence objected. "You'll be killed! You can't stop them with rifles!"

"No," he agreed. "Rifle cartridge isn't much good against those milking stools. But all I have to do is linger here, and my shadow'll take care of the rest." A brilliant streak of lightning lit the canyon. The rain came down in a torrent.

"The storm, Mr. Gibson!" Joshua was tugging at Clarence's shirt, desperate to get him to understand. "It's the twister that follows him, snatching up the souls of the damned to Hell! We have to run!"

Clarence shoved Joshua off angrily and turned to plead with his brother. "Caleb, for God's sake!"

"Don't be thick now, Clarence. You saw what I did. You see what I'm doing now. I ain't Caleb no more. Listen to young Mr. Cobb and get the folks out of here."

The wind whipped furiously and a steady cannonade of thunderbolts shook the walls of the canyon. The man who was Caleb Gibson looked behind him to the black sky and grinned. "It was good to see you again, brother, but it's time to go. My shadow's here."

The Lights Go Out

Captain Sheldrake's great round face thrust out from the doorway, his eyes darting, his red cheeks quivering. An impatient gust from his lungs set his push-broom mustache billowing. "Hurry, God damn you!"

But Professor Addison Lang couldn't possibly hurry any more than he already was. He had lost his shoe and now his right foot left a trail of blood on the glass-strewn cobblestones. Out of breath and beyond hope, he dragged himself to the stone arch with what seemed to him to be dreamlike slowness. Indeed, the world itself seemed to be an opium delirium, a nightmare from which he desperately hoped to wake. He collapsed panting against the wall, and by turns the panting became weeping. Lang became aware of a distant whistling, increasingly shrill in pitch, rising over his sobs, but to this fact he assigned no importance.

Sheldrake surged at him, his face contorted in a furious rage. The old cavalryman's huge hands caught him by the collar and yanked him off his feet. Lang only bawled the more at the assault. Couldn't Sheldrake allow him this moment to grieve, or had the Afghan caves and the hills of the Punjab eaten his last shred of compassion?

Lang flew through the air, struck flat with his shoulders against the wet brick wall of the inner chamber. His head rang like a bell, and he tasted blood in his mouth. As he slowly regained his senses, he saw Sheldrake through a cloud of brown dust, coughing violently and swaying on his knees as he tried to stand.

Lang's own pants and coat were run through with holes and his heavy satchel was shredded; his books and all else of importance in his life that could be saved littered the floor. Only belatedly did Lang realize that Sheldrake was not assaulting him, but trying to pull him to safety. His stunned brain laboriously arrived at the conclusion that an errant artillery shell had landed in the lane outside.

'So we're finally fighting back,' he thought. He was not bitter that the trifling effort at defiance nearly resulted in his death. At least the shock had stopped his sobbing.

He moved over to help up Captain Sheldrake, but the rotund old soldier shoved him out of the way. Sheldrake's lips moved but it was impossible to hear him. Mechanically, Lang walked back to his pile of belongings and gathered them up: Newton's Principia, volumes of Milton and Chaucer, his family's ancient King James, and a copy of Dante, stained from the bottle of laudanum that had just been smashed on it. This last loss elicited a sharp curse.

While the professor gathered up his possessions, Sheldrake lumbered over to the circular vault door and pulled on its great brass wheel. Lang heard the ratcheting of the locks as thin clicks through his buzzing ear drums. A draft of cold air with a vague antiseptic scent flowed out of the opening portal. He glanced up at plaque on the side of the door: "NO ADMITTANCE. PRIVATE PASSAGE FOR GRAND LODGE MEMBERS ONLY."

Lang's stomach rolled at the thought of stepping through the portal, and what it meant for that door to close and the walls of a whole universe to close with it. At first, he had thought the building of the redoubts was eccentricity, then lunacy, and finally hard-headed prudence, though he never dreamed that he would have to flee to one himself.

Sheldrake waved him through. Lang limped to the door, giving the blue skies and green hills of earth one final look. His fingers brushed the engraved plaque, and he thought they ought to have added to it the phrase: "Abandon all hope."

It was two hours later when the physician treated his wounds and dispensed a new bottle of laudanum. That is to say two hours had passed by the count of his timepiece; Lang recalled Sir Dunstan Penrose's presentation to the committee about how the passage of time may not be constant across all that horrifying kaleidoscope of invisible worlds the Exploratory Corps called the Empyrean. How everyone howled at the suggestion! But now the possibility made Lang's skin crawl.

"Which one," Lang began, pursing his flustered lips and gesticulating to replace the words he could not say. Finally, he managed to ask: "Where are we?"

The orderly raised his eyes from the process of bandaging Lang's foot. "Which redoubt? Is that what you mean, sir?"

Lang nodded.

"Fortress Tintagel, sir."

"And where is Fortress Tintagel?"

The orderly's brow creased in thought. "I don't know that I can rightly answer that, sir. Perhaps the Lord Marshall can better explain it to you, sir. At the gathering this cycling."

"Cycling?" Lang growled. "What the hell is a cycling?"

"Your pardon, sir. There's no night or day here, properly called. We mark time according to the cycle of the color of the astral vapor, from Amber to Azure to Violet. The period is perfectly regular. Right now it is Azure, sir."

A strained and fretful smile passed across Lang's face, and then he bit his lip lest it turn into delirious laughter. He felt a very tenuous hold on his sanity, and feared that at any moment it might slip away.

The period of time called Azure passed without descent into hysteria, and the first bell of Violet brought him limping on crutches to the cavernous auditorium along with Sheldrake and three score other strangers, most looking as tattered and bedraggled as he was.

Lang was astonished to see dozens of women and children in the crowd. Even with the outlandish charters adopted by some of the order's foreign lodges, the rolls of the Wise Knights of the Enlightenment were only open to men, and then only those of an age that would admit some measure of distinction and accomplishment. It took him some time to puzzle out this mystery, though the answer should have immediately presented itself: these were the wives and children of his fellow knights. The realization was disconcerting.

Was this not the purpose of the redoubts? Of course he knew that, knew it before the foundation stones of the first Void Fortress were laid, but only now did he comprehend the gravity of that fact. For the first time he fully understood that their removal to this impossible place was for an unlimited duration. The Wise Knights had abandoned the earth; he would not see it again in his lifetime.

On an elevated lectern stood the Lord Marshall in full regalia of the order. Encircling him were a half dozen others, crisply dressed in uniform of the Exploratory Corps or the military cohorts. They were young and old, but all very dour.

Without preface, the Lord Marshall spoke: "Wise Knights, this is the hour we have dreaded. For seven hundred years, we have awaited the prophesied Age of Enlightenment. The dawn broke but now has passed. The lights are going out."

The declaration provoked a lot of murmuring and more than one angry outburst. In the midst of the commotion, Lang squinted, trying to make out the face of the Lord Marshall in the purple-tinged light that filtered through the great crystalline canopy above. His eyes widened in recognition. "My God! It's Penrose!"

Annoyed, Sheldrake hushed him.

"I assumed he was dead," Lang said.

"You assumed incorrectly," was Sheldrake's curt reply.

"He looks just as he did when last I saw him. That was a quarter century ago," Lang intoned. Penrose had been right about the differential in the passage of time. Lang's forehead beaded with sweat and his mouth dried up at the thought of how many ages would pass in the outside world while he hid in Tintagel.

A strident American voice rose above the clamor, interrupting his thought: "We must counter-attack! Haven't we the means, after all this time?"

Another with a Russian accent concurred: "Let us strike before they can gain a lodgment on the earth! Why wait until they gather their strength?"

"The enemy is already too strong, and we are too few!" declaimed the Lord Marshall. "What we protect here – your lives, our knowledge – is too precious to be wasted on vainglory. The entire future of our race hinges on our weathering this storm. For now, the gates of Tintagel are shut."

"This is surrender!"

Lang was surprised to discover that it was he who cried out. A dozen other voices cheered his courage, but in truth it was a vent of maddened desperation. Lang lacked the mettle for war; he would avail the Wise Knights nothing in battle, but the thought of never seeing the sun rise, of never hearing the waves crash or the sky thunder was too much to bear.

One of the knights clad in military vestments raised his voice above the commotion. "Wise Knights, earth is lost! The redoubts are our home now!"

The Lord Marshall nodded. "These are our walled abbeys on the fringe of the wilderness, and we are the cloistered monks guarding the last flame of civilization until such time as we may carry it back to what remnant of our race perseveres, if any. Wise Knights, this is the new dark age. The flame gutters, but it has not yet gone out. We will keep it burning if we may, but our order must be reforged for the task.

"Even to the days of our forefathers, we have been scholars and bookworms: librarians, physicians, taxonomists, alchemists, and astronomers. We have been scribblers, calculators, and spell casters. Scholarship and inquiry has served us well. It has brought us this far, but it will bring us no farther."

At this remark, silence descended on the whole assembly. Outside, the stars – or whatever queer orbs kindled the heavens in this uncanny place – flared brilliantly, casting a grave shadow across the face of

Lord Marshall Penrose. In that alien light he looked lordly and terrible indeed.

"Our place at the summit of creation was a maiden aunt's fancy. The universe is hostile; we were fools to think it could ever be tamed by intellect alone. But long ago we were knights in more than just name. We were lions before we were sheep! If we endure, then we must become lions again!

"If we had been more martial and valorous, as inclined to strength in arms as to strength in mind, we might not now be hiding in the Empyrean while the spiderish hordes of Mars sack our world. I pray God that we may one day return the favor, but that mighty task must be left to our children and our children's children. For the rest of us, the dream of the golden dawn is dead; only our posterity will be fit to take it up again.

"Yesterday, we were knights of Enlightenment. Today we are naught but knights of the cold void. Yet knights we remain! Let us not forget it."

Appendix - The Signalman

Jamison Doyle (1873-1952), popularly known as the Signalman, was one of the most important metahuman heroes of the War of the Worlds. While working as a railway signalman on the Severn Valley Line during the opening days of the Martian invasion, he encountered a wounded Eldil while trying to warn off a refugee train set to be derailed. For his valor and compassion, the Supernal bestowed three Lenses on Jamison, making him the first human *Celestial Paladin* of the modern age.

After the defeat of the Martians, Doyle remained a highly influential and admired figure, becoming a prominent, if accidental, spokesman for the rights of industrial workers and Irish independence, as well as a foe of the British Republican government. He would continue to battle supernatural and mundane threats throughout his life, and he received great acclaim among the Paladins, eventually obtaining the rank of Astral Warden. He spent the last decade of his life in seclusion, and it is said that he was afflicted with Stigmata.

A devout Catholic, he was canonized in 1997 with nine confirmed miracles attributed to his intervention. He is a patron saint of railroad workers and passengers, astronauts, and Talents.

Gallery

Signalman

Cyclone Ranger

The Fey

About the Ascension Epoch

Ascension Epoch is a shared universe for original fiction. It was originally created by Mike and Shell DiBaggio as a setting for their superhero and adventure stories, built around an alternate history that incorporates many details from public domain literature, movies, and comic books. All of the stories, characters, and artwork are open source, licensed under a Creative Commons Attribution-ShareAlike license, meaning anyone is free to reshare or create derivative works, even for profit, as long as they credit the original creators and link back to our site. The setting was built to encourage collaboration with other writers and artists. To learn more, please visit our website http://www.ascensionepoch.cc

Enjoy the Book? Let us Know!

Few things make Mike and Shell happier than hearing from people who enjoyed their work. Feel free to contact them on the web at ascensionepoch.com or by email at mike@ascensionepoch.com or shellpresto@ascensionepoch.com.

If you really want to make their day, then leave a review wherever you purchased this book, and then tell all your friends about us! You can 'Like' our Facebook page, circle us on Google Plus, and talk us up on Twitter with the #AscensionEpoch tag.

About the Creators

Mike and Shell are a husband and wife team whose love for storytelling began with an early passion for superhero comics, SF/Fantasy novels, and role playing games. When they're not writing or illustrating, they can often be found hiking, building Legos, customizing action figures, or watching old horror movies. They live in St. Clair, Pennsylvania, along with their three dogs and two cats.

Made in the USA
Middletown, DE
20 October 2022

13104099R00027